⑤ 6/01
3/03 ⑧ LAD 3/02

Green Tales

GREEN TALES

Written and illustrated by

Béatrice Tanaka

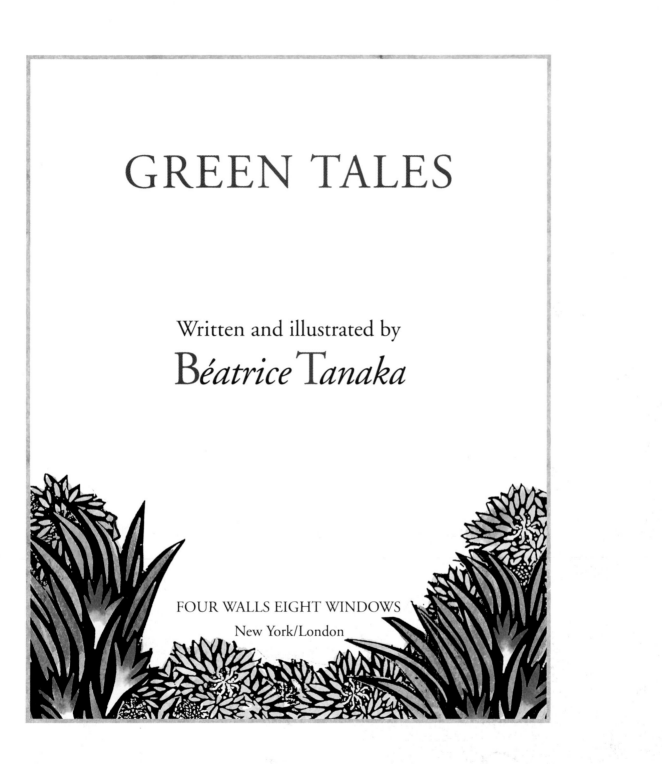

FOUR WALLS EIGHT WINDOWS

New York/London

Illustrations and text © 1994 Béatrice Tanaka

Published by: Four Walls Eight Windows
39 West 14th Street, #503, New York, New York, 10011

U.K. Offices: Four Walls Eight Windows/Turnaround
27 Horsell Road, London, N51 XL, England

First printing June 1994.

Library of Congress Cataloging-in-Publication Data:
Green Tales/ illustrated and written by Béatrice Tanaka.
p.   cm.
Contents: The sowers—Tané of the forests—Yggdrasil—Happiness—
The tree of darkness—How people came to be—The buffalo—The milk of mercy.
Summary: Eight myths from around the world on an ecological theme.
ISBN: 1-56858-020-7
1. Creation—Folklore—Juvenile literature. 2. Tales. [1. Creation—folklore. 2. Folklore.]
I. Title.
PZ8.1.T154Gr   1993
398.21—dc20   93-16291
                                               CIP
                                               AC

Printed in Hong Kong

To the memory of Albert Botbol
gardener of souls

Table of Contents

The Sowers   9

Tané of the Forests   13

Yggdrasil   22

Happiness   25

The Tree of Darkness   33

How People Came to Be   37

The Buffalo   42

The Milk of Mercy   47

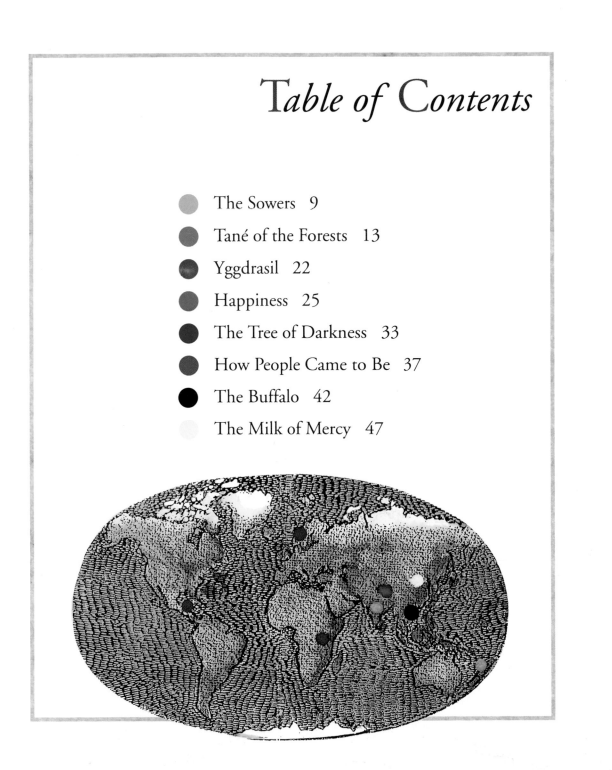

The Sowers

INDIA

From their lofty abode, Mahadev and Gauri gazed at the boundless space surrounding them. Suddenly, they noticed a tiny planet far below, all bare and empty. Their hearts throbbed with compassion. Carrying seeds from their heavenly garden, they dove into space. And as they descended from the swirling stars, they grew heavier and denser in the ever-thicker air.

A young man and woman look searchingly at the cracked, pebbly soil they have just landed on. Above them, a yellow sun rolls slowly in a desert sky.

"Go eastward, and plant a seed at each step. I shall do likewise, heading westward," says the young man.

His companion smiles and turns towards the east. She stoops, digs a small hole, drops a seed into it, covers the hole, rises, goes a step farther, stoops again.

When she turns to look at her companion, he has become a distant outline.

A step. A seed. A step.

The sun weighs like lead on her bent back.

The young woman straightens and glances over her shoulder.

The small outline is only a wavering point on the horizon.

A seed. A step... A seed...

On turning around for the third time, the young man is gone; but a track of green sprouts joins their steps over the plain.

She stoops again, digs a small hole...

A drop of salty water falls into it with the seed.

The sun blazes and disappears behind the newly-born saplings.

It rises in front of the young woman.

Then sets behind the young trees.

The woman continues walking.

Stooping.

Planting.

She knows that someone does the same work elsewhere. That they move away from each other and yet come nearer again, step by step, seed by seed.

They lose track of the days, the months and years through which they keep walking.

They have forgotten their aching backs.

They do not notice the hardness of the soil anymore: their hands have become hardened and cracked, too.

They repeat the same movements endlessly.

Slowly. Patiently. Silently.

All they know now are steps. Holes. Seeds.

And sun. Soil. Loneliness.

And the green track which rustles softly as it lengthens and spreads behind them.

The old woman covers the seed she has just sown.

A shadow falls on her brown, withered hand.

She lifts her tired lids and stares at the quiet old man whose eyes fix hers.

"Who are you?" she hears herself ask, and thinks her own voice sounds strange, almost like a stranger's.

"Mahadev..." slowly answers the man, as if the words reached him from far, far away. "And you are Gauri, my companion..."

"We have finished our task. We can go home," he says.

Hand in hand, they rise into the air. And as they ascend, their backs straighten, their wrinkles disappear, their bodies become weightless, turn into flame and light.

Below, a sea of plants waving their leaves like so many goodbye handkerchiefs disappears behind the brand-new clouds.

From the boundless skies, Mahadev and Gauri gaze at a tiny planet, green and blue.

The Earth.

Tané of the Forests

Before the beginning, in times before time, Father Rangi the Sky and Mother Pappa the Earth were quite close, so fondly enlaced that no light ever reached their children. Tané of the Forests, Tangaroa the Ocean, Tao-hiri-matea the Wind and their siblings grew up crawling in their warm shadow, pale and numbed under Rangi's black weight.

"We're too cramped!" protested Tangaroa, trying to stretch his watery limbs.

"We're not tiny toddlers clinging to their mother!" shouted fiery Tu-mata-uenga, heaving desperately.

"I feel something wonderfully sweet beyond Father, something strange that calls and draws me upwards," mused Tané, twisting in his effort to straighten and shoot up.

"I can't stand it anymore! We must take action, and quickly, too!" cried Tangaroa.

"Let us kill them," proposed Tu-mata-uenga.

"Never!" said Tané. "Do you forget they are our parents?"

"But they oppress us!"

"Then let us separate them. Let's scare off Rangi and stay with Mother Earth."

"No, no and no!" hissed Tao-hiri-matea the Wind. "Rangi the Sky is our father. He protects us."

"He may protect you, who flutter about at his feet. But what about us? He forbids us to move. He forces us to grope about in darkness. He prevents our growing!" cried the others.

And without listening anymore to Tao-hiri-matea, Rongo of the Fields and Orchards pushed his large shoulders against the Sky.

Rangi's embrace did not slacken, as if he were unaware of his son's efforts.

"Let me try," said Tangaroa the Ocean.

He rose violently. He rolled and tossed his hugest waves until he fell back, exhausted.

"I'll do it!" roared Tu-mata-uenga, hitting the darkness overhead with his fists till his arms dropped with weariness.

And the Sky continued to weigh heavily on Earth and on her children.

Then Tané of the Forests moved forward. He lay down on his back, took a deep breath, propped his feet against Rangi, braced his legs and pushed.

Slowly.

Stubbornly.

With all the force of the life pulsing in his green veins...

14

A shiver went through Sky and Earth, turned into a moan, a cry, a roar. Their embrace slackened, then broke up. An eddy of light rushed into the void between their open hands, their parted bodies. Rangi, flung into space, started whirling ever farther away. Nameless distance swallowed his voice. Only his tears still bound him to Earth.

This was the very first rain.

Naked under the jewel-like droplets, Earth looked even more beautiful than her children had imagined.

"And I'll make you more lovely yet!" said Tané.

He covered her rounded hills with deep, green forests.

He adorned her valleys with countless sweet-smelling flowers.

He embellished her with butterflies and many-hued birds.

Then he looked towards the faraway, lonely Sky.

His heart was sad.

"I only separated you to allow life to blossom, but I love both of you. Just wait a little while, Father, and you'll see," he whispered.

And he went to work.

He created the sun as a breastplate for Rangi the Sky.

He made the moon and hung it over his father's back.

He went beyond the edge of the universe to bring him the purple-fringed twilight cloak.

And then he travelled even farther, towards the unknown spaces where Earth is only a dim recollection, to the country of Uru of the World's End.

"I had to separate our mother and father, but on moonless nights they are so sad... Couldn't you lend me some of your children to cheer them up?" he asked.

"I'll gladly send them," said Uru.

He clapped his hands, and from everywhere the Shining Ones came running, rolling and skipping joyously like so many laughing eyes. Uru filled a basket of woven light up to the rim with them, and Tané ran to bring them to his father. He asked four Shining Ones to hold the corners of the Sky's large cloak. He placed Five others in its center, like a shimmering cross. Then he scattered the rest over Rangi's vast body, and covered them with the basket of woven light so they would not fall off. If you don't believe this, just look at what is called the Southern Cross and the Milky Way; and if you keep very, very quiet, you may even hear the Shining Ones' crystalline laughter...

Then Pappa the Earth admired her faraway husband, and Rangi smiled at his wife, and Tané rejoiced in their joy.

But Tao-hiri-matea the Wind, who had followed his father into space, was jealous of this quiet happiness. Bitter and sullen, he waited until Tané had gone to rest in the heart of his forests, till Tangaroa the Ocean was busy playing with his grandchildren,

17

Ike-tere of the Fishes and Tu-te-wehi-wehi of the Reptiles. Then, whistling and roaring, his hands filled with thunderstones, he swooped down to Earth.

He whipped the ferns and beheaded the flowers. He broke twigs and branches, and rooted up the trees.

"Ho-hoo! Down with Tané and Tangaroa!" he shrieked, leaving a trail of waste and sorrow wherever he passed.

He took a sharp turn and began to chase the waves until their foam licked Rangi's feet and their whirlpools uncovered the deepest-lying reefs.

"Dive to the bottom of the Ocean!" cried Ike-tere to his children, the fishes.

"Let us rather take shelter on the beaches!" panicked Tu-te-wehi-wehi of the Reptiles.

"Cowards! May your scales be singed for this treason!" cursed Ike-tere.

"May those who fulfill your wish pursue you even in the deepest waters!" answered Tu-te-wehi-wehi, fleeing inland.

"Ho-hooo!" exulted Tao-hiri-matea. "I wreaked havoc on Tané's work, I trampled Rongo and Haumie's children, I destroyed the mighty Tangaroa and pitted his grandchildren against each other! Nobody can hold out against me, nobody..."

"I do," proudly asserted Tu-mata-uenga.

"On your knees, impudent dwarf!" roared the Wind.

"Try to force me down, you who dared forsake your mother!" cried Tu-mata-uenga.

19

Tao-hiri-matea quivered with rage. He threw himself against his young brother. He jostled him. He shook him wildly. He blew, he bellowed, he roared and raged and stormed…

But Tu-mata-uenga faced him, straight and unmoved, until the breathless Wind drew back and returned to his home near Rangi.

"I am the strongest! The children of Tané and Tanagaroa, and of Rongo and of Haumie-tike-tike are at my feet! For now and forever they will be my children's servants!" triumphed Tu-mata-uenga, on seeing the scattered plants and the frothy sea.

Only Tu-mata-uenga had no children.

Tané put the broken trees upright and created new ones, and Rongo and Haumie-tike-tike did likewise with the grasses, the banana-trees and the ferns. Tu-te-wehi-wehi's reptilian children learned to live in their shade, which they shared with the returning birds and butterflies. Tangaroa smoothed his bedraggled waves and tried to forget his grandchildren's quarrel.

And Rangi the Sky smiled at Pappa the Earth, who was lovelier than ever before.

It was at that time that Tané felt something was missing in Creation. He looked at the reddish clay at his feet and called his immortal siblings. Together they shaped a being in the likeness of their mother, with a hill-like, rounded body, with river-like flowing hair and eyes deep as mountain lakes. Tané bent down

20

and breathed into its nostrils, and lo! it was no more an earthen likeness, but a living woman: Hine-ma-onu, who became Tané's gentle wife, his daughters' mother.

"Aha! So that's how I'll get a son!" thought Tu-mata-uenga, and he hurriedly carved a stone in his own likeness: Tiké, the first man.

"I give you power over all creation!" said Tu-mata-uenga, and he taught his son how to build houses and canoes, and how to cut down Haumie-tike-tike's ferns to make a bed. He showed Man how to reap fruits and cereals, the children of Rongo-ma-tane, and how to singe the scales of Tu-te-wehi-wehi's descendants, the reptiles, so as to make meals tastier.

Then Tangaroa the Ocean remembered the reptiles' long-ago flight, and rose angrily onto the beaches to take them back to their old home; and Tiké the Man, on seeing his fields flooded, got into his canoe to chase the waves and to trap Tangaroa's children's children...

"This is the curse of the day of my victory!" said Tu-mata-uenga, on telling his son how he had fought Tao-hiri-matea the Wind. And he unveiled unto him the secret of his name: Tu-mata-uenga, War.

Hundreds and thousands of years have passed since that day. But in spite of the efforts of their wives, the daughters of Tané and Hine-ma-onu the Gentle, Tiké and his sons seem unable to forget the name of their ancestor.

Yggdrasil
VIKING, SCANDINAVIA

There exists an evergreen ashtree, immeasurable as the universe. Its roots burrow into unknown depths. Its leafy crown is the sky itself. A keen-sighted eagle lives there, and nothing escapes his always open eyes.

Three lone women sit in the ashtree's shadow. Childless, ageless, loveless, the Norns are the servants of the Great Law, the Sovereigns of Fate. Day and night they spin, weave and cut the life-thread of all creation.

A brook flows at their feet. Its crystal-clear waters whiten everything they touch. It provides the dew with which the Norns water the ashtree's branches; for should even a single twig wither or rot, a world would collapse and disappear.

Three immense roots hold up the tree. One leads to the fathomless, snakefilled abyss, where a dragon gnaws at it unceasingly.

The second root leads to the Frost Giants' home, where the Spring of Wisdom sings softly in the wilderness.

The third root leads to the Assembly of the Gods, the Sons of Light, past the rainbow-bridge watched over by Heimdal the White One.

Up and down the tree-trunk, from the top where the eagle dwells to the infernal depths where the dragon growls, runs a squirrel-messenger. He carries threats from the one to the other, and keeps track of the countless days and ages which separate the present from the end of Time.

For the Twilight of the Gods is marked in the Norns' weaving.

On that far-off day, Heimdal will dig up the horn buried between the three roots. The shrill notes of the horn will awaken the living and the dead. It will call them to the Great Battle between the Powers of Darkness and the Guardians of Light. Demons and dread creatures will break loose. The sun will darken. Fire will ravage the plain, and raging waves will batter the highest mountaintops.

But if mankind does not side with the evil trolls and snakes that lie in wait in the dark, the tree will stand firm. And when at last the bloody waters of battle recede, the tree will grow, a brighter, truer green, on an earth blessed by peace and everlasting spring.

Happiness

Long ago, a lush forest covered the foothills of the Highest Mountains. Nestled in the forest there lay a most happy little kingdom. Its crops were more bountiful, its springs and rivers clearer, its people friendlier than anywhere else. "Thief" and "beggar" were unknown words, and nobody remembered having ever witnessed a quarrel. When he heard about it, the ruler of the neighboring country could hardly believe such a place existed; but once he had made sure it did exist, he promptly sent an ambassador to ask about the origin of this extraordinary peace and prosperity.

Now the ambassador—as any courtier would—thought that only the king of the happy kingdom could answer his master's question.

And the king—as any king would—felt so flattered and proud that he said:

"Does your gracious sovereign ignore that a country's happiness springs from its ruler's wisdom, as a valley's fruitfulness derives from the river that irrigates its fields?"

The ambassador definitely did not like these words.

And the king's counselors liked them even less.

"If it weren't for my careful management, the country would certainly be less prosperous!" grumbled the royal treasurer on coming home.

"If it weren't for my courage in defending its borders, the country would surely be less peaceful!" growled the king's general, banging his door.

"If it weren't for my reading Heaven's decrees, His Majesty would boast less about his royal wisdom!" frowned the astrologer.

Of course their families repeated these words to their friends. Who told their kinsmen. Who discussed them at home and on the marketplace. In no time, the whole town talked only about the ambassador's question, the king's answer, and his counselors' opinions, and every man, woman and child commented on the story. Each and all insisted that he—or she—was also responsible for the country's happiness, and quite right they were on that point. But on wishing to show in what way and how much so, they started arguing; and as one cannot argue and do one's work at the same time, they forgot to till their fields, or care for their households, or learn their lessons. Soon everybody was angry and

yelling at everybody else, and the happiness they talked so much about was nowhere to be found.

On meeting one week later, the entire royal council looked thin and pale.

"Bad times," muttered the astrologer.

"Awful times," snorted the treasurer.

"Terrible times," sputtered the general. "Two of my officers even started a fight because of that cursed question-monger. If only I could lay hands on him, I'd gladly shorten him by a headlength!"

"The head of an ambassador is sacred," observed the king.

"And anyway, our visitor has vanished. He said his question had become useless," added the astrologer.

A heavy silence followed. It was only broken at dusk, when a young servant girl brought His Excellency's tea. But instead of leaving the council-hall on tiptoe, as was the custom from time immemorial, she turned on the threshold and said:

"When the mighty ones lose their way, sometimes a shepherd can find it. And right now we humble folks believe you should go and see the Old Man of the Forest and ask his advice!"

And so troubled was the king that, instead of scolding her insolence, like the general, or her bad manners, like the treasurer, or her superstitions, like the astrologer, he just nodded and said:

"By my royal seal, that's a deal! Gentlemen, be ready by daybreak tomorrow!"

Nobody knew the Old Man's true name, nor his age, nor what bustling village or town he had left on coming to live in the woods. But as the years had gone by, his frail figure and his radiant eyes had become part of the landscape, like the gnarled boles of the trees or the quiet twinkling of the stars.

He met his magnificent visitors in front of his little hut. He listened to them with a smile. And then he bade them follow him, on foot and without their retinue.

Soon creepers and thorns hid their path. The sun's clear rays turned into a greenish twilight beneath the thick tangle of the forest. Strange noises filled the moist air. The king and his counselors stumbled over hidden roots, fell into moss-covered brooks, and would gladly have turned back, even without any answer to their question; but they did not know the way, and their guide seemed deaf to their sighs and groans, and hopped cheerfully along his invisible trail without ever turning around.

Breathless, ragged and soaking wet, the country's rulers suddenly found themselves in a clearing.

And lo!

In front of them, golden in the sunshine and starry with many-hued fruits and flowers, there stood a giant tree, and, in its shadow, the strangest living pyramid: a tiny bird atop

a rabbit astride a monkey sitting on an elephant, each picking fruit to share with his neighbor...

The Old Man greeted the animals, sat down by their side, and asked his visitors to do likewise. And when they had quenched their thirst with the juicy berries, he said:

"Many years ago, when this tree bore its first fruit, these four, who look so friendly now, came running angrily to my hut.

"'Tell those thieves to leave my tree alone!' each yelled as loudly as possible.

"'Why does each of you think the tree is his alone?' I asked.

"'Because I watered it whenever the rains were late!' bellowed the elephant.

"'Because I kept watch so no boar or deer would hurt it when it was a sapling!' screeched the monkey.

"'Because I pulled out the weeds which threatened to strangle it when it was a seedling!' piped the rabbit.

"'Because I planted its seed which I brought from a faraway island...and yet I only ask to nibble at some of its fruit,' chirped the bird.

"Ashamed, the others bowed their heads, and asked the bird to alight at the top of their pyramid, so as to show the tree that they all loved it with one heart. And out of joy to see its four friends thus united, the tree flowered again with rainbow-colored blossoms, whose sweet perfume and blissful rustling spread over the whole countryside."

"Whose happiness, therefore, springs from here, the heart of the forest!" exclaimed the king in wonder.

"And I suppose it will return once everybody has seen this strange circle of friends," mused the astrologer.

"We'd just have to build a good road for all these pilgrims," said the treasurer.

"And put some men at every crossroad to show the right way," added the general.

"So the crowds would arrive in a clearing of down-trodden grass and a golden fence protecting the tree and its comrades?" bantered the Old Man.

"Ah... Hmm... Hum..." muttered the embarrassed counselors.

The king wrinkled his brow, thinking very hard indeed.

"If I hadn't seen all this myself, I would not believe it; so how can I ask my people to believe this wonder without seeing it?" he asked.

"Your Majesty could have paintings of this scene done on silk and on paper, and the peddlers selling them would carry the story to the farthest ends of the country, and even beyond," proposed the Old Man of the Forest.

"By my royal seal, that's a deal!" exclaimed the king...

And he kept his word.

Only, as time went by, peddlers and storytellers became rare and rarer; so that, nowadays, almost nobody remembers this tale.

The Tree of Darkness

DJAGGA, AFRICA

At first, nobody paid attention to the tiny seedling in the shadow of the cliff, near the river.

Nobody noticed its strangely quick growth, like a giant mushroom's.

Nobody knew it was Nridosi.

It soared ever higher. It spread ever farther. Soon its crown hid the sky.

A deep shadow covered the sun.

Without dawn or twilight, moon or stars, time stood still.

And madness seized the earth.

Lions and hyenas ran howling through the village.

Banana-boughs turned into serpents. Little billy-goats became dreadful wild beasts. Doorways grew sharp fangs.

And Nridosi's roots lengthened like live ropes. They crept silently along the paths between the huts. They wormed their way through cracks and crannies, searching for throats to throttle, for necks to break.

Only children could brave this dread night, by beating the wizard tree with swords too heavy for their small hands. Then the creeping roots would fall back a little, allowing the children to search for clay to fill up the cracks in the walls, for food and firewood.

And still Nridosi soared and spread. It was everywhere. It seemed to fill the universe, and in the darkness the air became ever heavier, more rotten...

"It has grown too tall," said the village elders.

"Maybe it is dead, and only its gigantic body keeps it from tumbling down."

"Someone should try to cut it down, so the sun can come back!"

"Only a child can do this."

"Maybe..."

Nobody remembers the name of the child.

Stumbling over the long, now motionless roots, the elders brought the child to the rim of the cliff.

Groping in the dark, they wrapped an ox-skin around its frail body, tied a rope to it, then lowered it slowly to the foot of the wizard tree.

Balancing on the slippery stones, the child swung its large sword and struck at the darkest darkness. The weapon sunk into the flabby night. Slimy liquid squirted out, gurgling.

The child staggered, recovered its foothold, lifted the sword and struck once more.

And again.

Again.

Again...

And suddenly the immense trunk shivered and collapsed into dust.

The light came back, though the river ran red under the sun.

But the sky was blue again, and the birds sang, and the wind blew, soft and fresh...

And all the trees stretched their branches to the sun, sprouted leaves and blossoms, and dripped with honey.

How People Came To Be
MAYA, MEXICO

In the abyss of time, surrounded by light in the midst of the dark
waters, the Great Ancestors decided to create the world.

"May the void be filled! May the waters recede! May Earth
appear, become dense and solid!" they said.

Immediately, like a cloud of dust, the mountains appeared
and rose towards the sky. And to break the silence floating around
them, the Sovereign Ancestors, Grandmother of Dawn and
Grandfather of Day gave form and life to birds and beasts,
the spirits of the ridges and guardians of the forest.

"Speak up! Sing to the Heart of Heaven! Praise the Plumed
Serpent, glorify your Mother's and your Father's name!" they
ordered.

But the beasts could only roar and bark, the birds could only
chirp and whistle. They had no words. They could not praise the
Sovereign Ancestors, and this is why they were condemned to be
hunted and eaten.

"Soon light will spread. Let us quickly create those who will invoke us!" said the Great Ancestors.

And they modeled speaking beings out of clay.

But clay is soft. The new creatures were limp. They collapsed and melted in the water, and although they could speak, their words made no sense.

The Creators kneaded them back into clay, and tried again by carving wood.

Their latest creatures looked human. They spoke. They hunted and cooked animals. They grew and multiplied. They built houses. They made pottery, they shaped weapons and jewels. But they had neither soul nor memory, and forgot their Creators.

The Heart of Heaven darkened. Black rain fell ceaselessly. Beasts and things rebelled.

"Let us devour those who hunted and ate us!" howled the animals, attacking their tormenters.

"Let us grind those who crushed us!" growled the millstones, whirling in the air.

"Let us burn those who put us into the fire!" cried the kitchen pots and the metal in the blacksmiths' shops, flying and swirling 'round like blazing birds.

And all rushed headlong at the forgetful creatures.

In vain the wooden beings tried to hide in deep caves and on treetops.

"Did you not destroy us and turn us into quarries? Did you not cut us down with your axes?" thundered the rocks and the trees, falling heavily on the escapees, while the waters rose and washed the earth clean of the woodmen with no soul or memory.

And in the dead of the once-again silent night, the Creators wondered:

"Out of what should we make thinking and thankful beings?"

At that very moment, Yac the mountain cat, Utiu the coyote, Quel the small parrot and Hoh the owl turned up. They came from Paxil and Cayala, the rich valleys flooded with nutritious mud. They showed the way to the land of the life-giving plants, of the golden-eared corn with its snow-colored grains.

The Sovereign Ancestors rejoiced. They gathered the silk-covered ears and picked off the white and yellow seeds. They ground and pressed them into nine drinks and a very smooth dough: the blood, the bones and the muscles of the first human beings.

And when they had finished their work, the Creators said:

"Look at the mountains, gaze at the green valleys, behold the world under the rising sun!"

The newcomers opened their eyes. They smiled and admired the happy land of Paxil with its countless fruits, the deep forests of Cayala blessed with honey. They bowed low and said:

"In truth, we thank you: for we are endowed with movement, with thought and with words. Glory be to you, Grandmother of Dawn, Grandfather of Day, for having created us, for bestowing

40

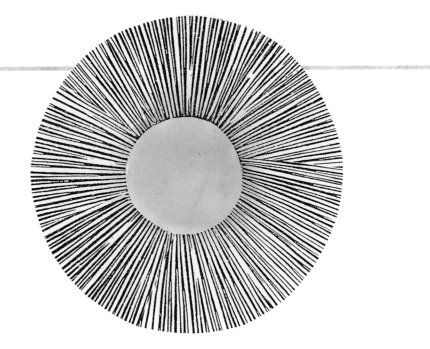

on us the knowledge of near and far, of the infinitely small on earth and the infinitely large in the skies!"

On hearing these praises, the Sovereign Ancestors changed their mind.

"If these creatures see everything under the sun, will they multiply? Will they not want to become our equals and break into the Heart of Heaven? May their sight be restricted to the face of the earth!"

Straightaway, like mist on a mirror, a thin veil fell over the eyes of the first humans.

Henceforth, they could only perceive what was near them.

But like the plant they were made of, the golden corn-mother rising towards the dazzling sun, they endeavor to look ever higher and farther.

The Buffalo
VIETNAM

The Heavenly Emperor had just created the seas and the mountains, man and woman, and most of the animals: then, wishing to provide food for all creatures, he shaped the seeds of the various cereals and grasses, and asked who, among his courtiers, would assume the task of sowing them.

"I will!" said Golden Light, pushing his way to the throne. As his name indicates, he was a star-spirit with a very brilliant face: but his brightness, unfortunately, went no farther than his figure.

However, since Golden Light had offered his services first, the Emperor had no choice but to entrust him with this most important office. Giving him the two kinds of seeds, Heaven said:

"First, you will sow the cereals you took in your right hand: on touching the soil, they will become rice and wheat, millet and corn, so man will have plenty. Then only will you scatter the grasses over the still empty fields: they are meant to nourish

42

the animals who, having four legs, can search for food in places far away. And please remember, don't mix the seeds!"

"No, Sir: first the cereals from my right hand and then the grasses from my left!" repeated the geni, bowing low. And then he left the place, flattered at the high office he was called to hold: for wasn't he putting the final touch to the Emperor's creation? He descended to earth, proudly carrying his big head and horned courtier's hat, swelling his brawny chest and strutting majestically towards a mountaintop, where he solemnly opened his hand...

Only he didn't know right from left!

The first grains to touch earth were the grasses and weeds, which now grew with terrifying speed, soon covering almost all the land. On seeing his mistake, Golden Light quickly scattered the cereal-seeds too: but there was almost no place for them, while the now big, strong weeds did their best to smother the tiny new plants.

On seeing his beautiful earth covered with hard, cutting grasses, the Emperor went pale with rage, and his voice echoed like a deep, sad bell through space:

"You conceited fool, who dared volunteer for a task you're unfit to do, thus ruining my work! Your place is no more at my side, but on the earth you spoiled, near man whose future you wrecked: I made him stand upright, his eyes among the stars, but because of your pride and ignorance, he'll be obliged to pass most of his life bent towards earth in his quest for food. Therefore, it is only just you help him till the soil and gain his livelihood.

You will push his plow and bow under his yoke, since you were too arrogant while sowing; you will obey even the smallest child, since you didn't listen to me; you will eat the bitter weeds you planted, and keep only the shining horns of your courtier's hat to remind you of your past..."

And this is how the buffalo was created.

If you don't believe this story, just look at his majestic, solemn gait, at his sad, nostalgic eyes, and the elegant horns he is still so proud of. Whenever he passes near a pond or a river, he will stop to admire his horns' reflection in the blue water: and the little buffalo-boy won't hurry him along, out of respect for his heavenly origin.

The Milk of Mercy

CHINA

In the beginning, only grasses covered the earth. Their ears were light as air, their grains so small one could not hull them. Our ancestors lived in hardship, and knew neither houses, nor fields, nor gardens.

Then Kwan Yin, the Goddess of Mercy, felt sorry for the poor humans. She came down to earth. For a whole long night she walked in the fields, pressing her motherly breast over the meager stalks; and every drop of her milk became a rounded, heavy, milky-white grain.

But oh, there were so many empty stalks!

Kwan Yin pressed her breasts until her milk mixed with blood...

And that is why, to this very day, white and red rice grows in the paddy-fields.